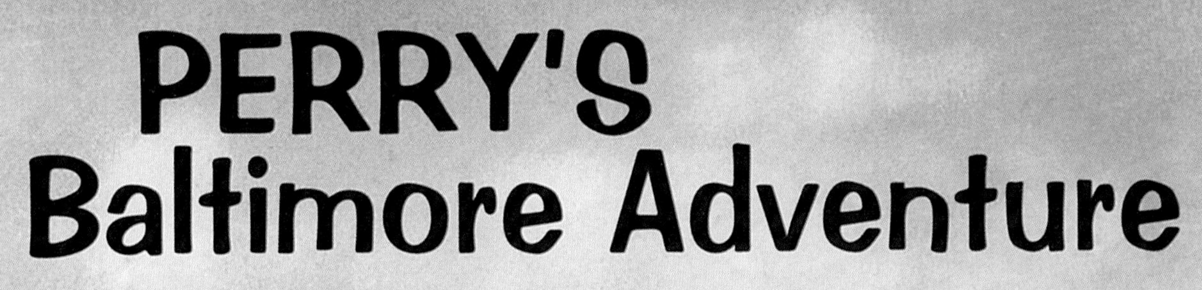

A BIRD'S-EYE VIEW OF CHARM CITY

Peter E. Dans

illustrated by
Kim Harrell

Camino Books, Inc.
Philadelphia

Once there was a lot of excitement in Baltimore, a place known as Charm City. A peregrine falcon had decided to live in the city, high on a ledge of a downtown skyscraper.

What made this so exciting? Well, not long ago, very few peregrine falcons were seen east of the Mississippi River. People had used a spray to keep bugs away from vegetables and other plants, but the spray was bad for

birds too. When everyone stopped using the spray, the falcons returned to the East Coast.

The people who saw the falcon in Charm City were very happy. They named the falcon Scarlett and helped build her a nest—a small, shallow tray which was filled with gravel so that eggs would not roll off the ledge.

After a while, a male peregrine falcon came to town. True to his name peregrine (which means wanderer), he had just finished a very long trip from South America to Baltimore and was ready to settle down. He landed on the same building where Scarlett lived, one floor above her nest. It was love at first sight. The people watching over Scarlett named the newcomer Beauregard.

The next year, everybody in Charm City was thrilled to learn that four eggs had been spotted in the falcons' nest. Scarlett and Beauregard took turns sitting on the eggs for four weeks until the chicks started to break out of their shells.

Like other peregrine falcons, Beauregard could see very far and dive very fast—over two hundred miles an hour. It was his job to get food for Scarlett and the hungry chicks. After diving between the buildings and along the harbor, he would come back with a wonderful feast.

The chicks would usually nap after they were fed, except Perry, who was very curious. Perry liked to climb to the edge of the nest and peek out at the world around him. Scarlett warned Perry to stay away from the edge of the nest because he might fall. Sure enough, one day, Perry got too close to the edge and started to tumble out.

In a flash, his mother rushed over and pushed Perry back into the nest. Scarlett gently scolded Perry for not listening to her.

Scarlett then promised Perry that if he was good and stayed away from the edge of the nest, his daddy would take him on a tour of Charm City as soon as he was able to fly.

Perry did everything he was told. He ate all his food, took his naps, and did flying exercises so he would be strong enough for his trip. He hopped around and

flapped his wings for ten minutes at a time. Sometimes, he would be up in the air for a few seconds, almost flying. Perry was causing such a commotion in the nest that his mother said he should do his exercises on the building's ledge. She told him to be careful not to fall off, but one day while Perry was practicing how to land, he skidded off the ledge.

Perry flapped his wings as fast as he could. He fell more than a hundred feet before he was able to gain control and fly to the ledge of a nearby building. Scarlett watched Perry land safely. She flew over to him and then followed him back to the nest.

When Beauregard returned with food for dinner, Scarlett told him what had happened. They agreed that it was time to keep their promise to Perry and take him on a tour of Charm City. So the next morning Beauregard and Perry said good-bye to the rest of the family and set out on their adventure.

Beauregard first flew over the harbor to show Perry the National Aquarium in Baltimore, where lots of colorful fish live. Here, children can enjoy watching dolphins, who put on a show every day.

The birds crossed the harbor and flew past the United States Navy ship *Constellation*, which was built over two hundred years ago.

The next stop was the Maryland Science Center,
where visitors can imagine traveling through time and

space to see the prehistoric world of dinosaurs or visit the planets and the stars.

Beauregard and Perry then flew to Fort McHenry where, during the War of 1812, Francis Scott Key saw the American flag flying and wrote the "Star-Spangled Banner." In 1931, this song became the National Anthem of the United States.

The birds then headed for Camden Yards, where the Baltimore Orioles play baseball.

Right next door they saw the stadium where the Baltimore Ravens play football.

A short flight brought them to the B&O Railroad Museum. Perry saw many wonderful old trains as well as the roundhouse, a very large building where train cars were built and repaired.

Then Beauregard and Perry flew over Mount Vernon Place and saw the monument honoring America's first president,

George Washington. They also saw many elegant homes, churches, and museums in the historic neighborhood.

As they flew over different parts of Baltimore, Beauregard told Perry about some of the famous people who once lived there.

Thurgood Marshall was the first African-American United States Supreme Court Justice.

Mother Seton was the first American-born person to be named a saint by the Catholic Church.

Edgar Allan Poe was famous for writing scary stories.

Babe Ruth was a great baseball player.

Johns Hopkins was the founder of a world-famous hospital and university.

Mary Pickersgill made the flag that flew over Fort McHenry when the British attacked Baltimore during the War of 1812.

Beauregard thought Perry should also know about some of the people who were not as famous but who helped to make the city charming.

Years ago, people called "arabbers" sold fruits and vegetables from wagons pulled by horses. A few of them are still seen in Charm City today.

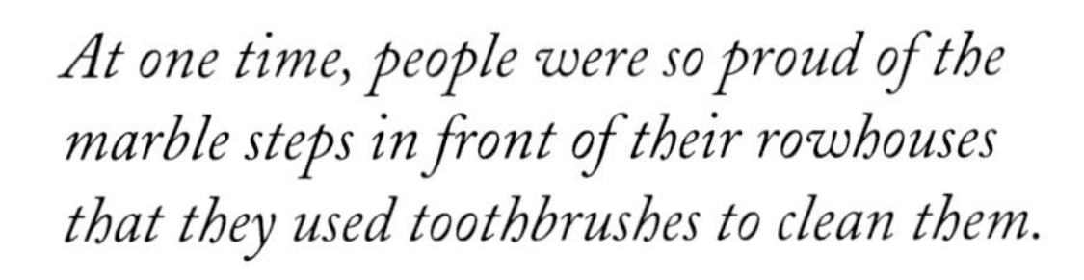

At one time, people were so proud of the marble steps in front of their rowhouses that they used toothbrushes to clean them.

Police Sergeant Bill and his horse Bob patrolled the streets of Baltimore.

Firemen waited for calls at the Number 6 Engine House, now a landmark in Old Town.

At the end of the day, Perry and Beauregard flew home. Perry was really, really tired. He ate a snack and went straight to bed. His sisters were very surprised because this was the first time he'd ever gone to bed before them.

While Perry slept, he dreamed about his great adventure. When he woke up, he thanked his parents and told them how glad he was to live in Baltimore. It truly *is* Charm City.